NBA
ON THE INSIDE

by James Buckley, Jr.

SCHOLASTIC INC.

New York   Toronto   London   Auckland   Sydney
Mexico City   New Delhi   Hong Kong   Buenos Aires

All photos copyright NBA, credit NBAE/Getty Images
Cover photo and title page photos:
Top Left: Andrew D. Bernstein
Top Right: Joe Murphy
Bottom: Andrew D. Bernstein

p. 3 — Gary Bassing; p. 4–5 — Juan Ocampo

p. 6 — Joe Murphy; p. 7 — Nathaniel S. Butler

p. 8 — Jesse D. Garrabrant; p. 9 — Jeff Reinking

p. 10 — Joe Murphy; p. 11 — Joe Murphy

p. 12–13 — Bill Baptist; p. 14 — Andrew D. Bernstein

p. 15 — Jeff Reinking; p. 16 — Noren Trotman

p. 17 — Andrew D. Bernstein; p. 18 — Allen Einstein

p. 19 — Gregory Shamus; p. 20 — Glenn James

p. 21 — Andrew D. Bernstein; p. 22–23 — Garrett Ellwood

p. 24–25 — Jennifer Pottheiser; p. 26 — Jesse D. Garrabrant

p. 27 — Mitchell Layton; p. 28 — Barry Gossage

p. 29 — Ron Turenne; p. 30 — Jeff Reinking

p. 31 — David Sherman; p. 32 — Barry Gossage

No part of this publication may be reproduced in whole or in part, or stored in a retrieval system or transmitted in any form or by any means, electronic, mechanical, photocopying, recording, or otherwise, without written permission of the publisher. For information regarding permission, write to Scholastic Inc., Attention: Permissions Department, 557 Broadway, New York, NY 10012.

The NBA and individual NBA member team identifications, photographs, and other content used on or in this publication are trademarks, copyrighted designs, and other forms of intellectual property of NBA Properties, Inc. and the respective NBA member teams and may not be used, in whole or in part, without the prior written consent of NBA Properties, Inc. All Rights reserved.

ISBN 0-439-57974-0

Copyright © 2003 by NBA Properties, Inc.
All rights reserved. Published by Scholastic Inc.
SCHOLASTIC and associated logos are trademarks and/or registered trademarks of Scholastic Inc.

12 11 10 9 8 7 6 5 4 3 2   4 5 6 7 8/0

Printed in the U.S.A.
First Scholastic printing, November 2003
Book Design: Louise Bova

YOUR ALL-ACCESS PASS TO THE NBA

You've watched NBA games on TV. You might have been to a game in person. But have you ever been in the locker room? Have you ever taken a ride on the team bus? Have you ever sat on the team bench and heard the coach call the plays? Unless you're a lot older (and taller!) than you look, you probably haven't done any of those things.

Until now!

Inside this book, take a behind-the-scenes look at life in the NBA. We'll take you places that you've never been before and show you how NBA players live and play at home and on the road. This is *NBA On the Inside*, and you've got a secret pass. Have a great time!

LOVE IT LIVE!

A full house at the Staples Center in Los Angeles is on hand for this game between the Portland Trail Blazers and the hometown Clippers. Millions of people attended NBA games during the 2002–03 season, and even more watched games on television.

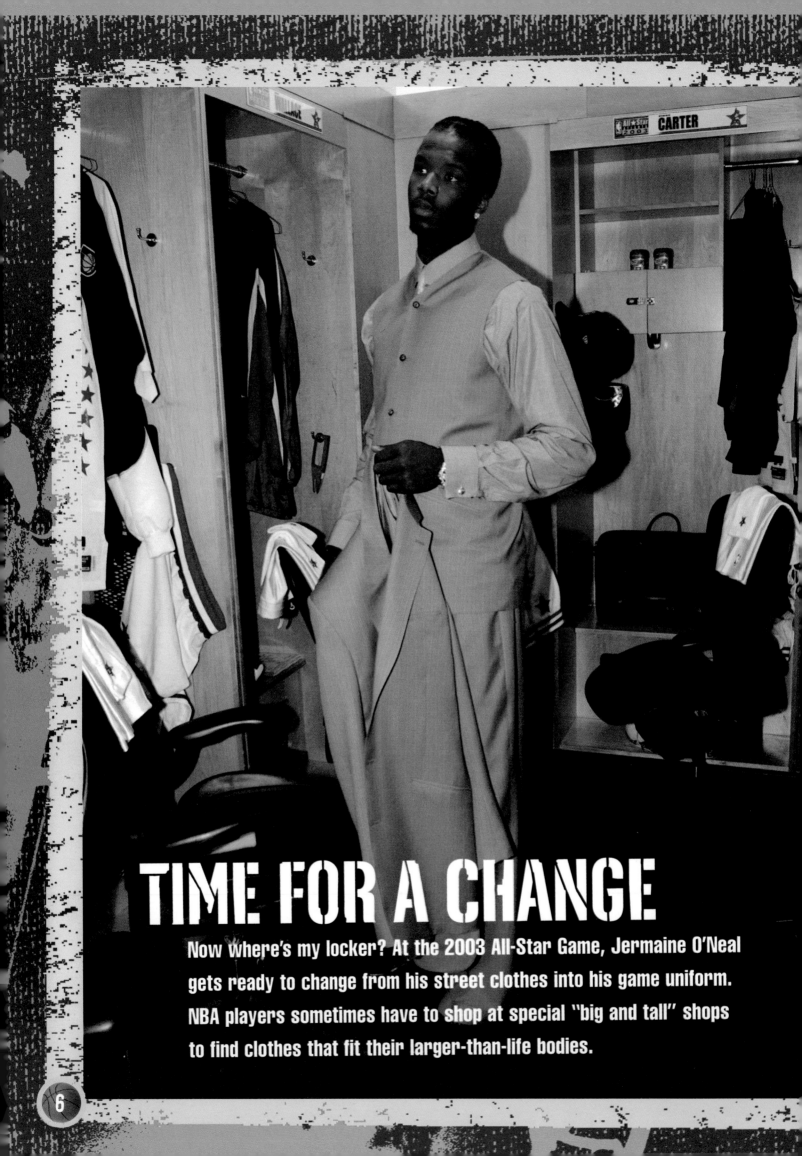

TIME FOR A CHANGE

Now where's my locker? At the 2003 All-Star Game, Jermaine O'Neal gets ready to change from his street clothes into his game uniform. NBA players sometimes have to shop at special "big and tall" shops to find clothes that fit their larger-than-life bodies.

REMOTE CONTROL

NBA players are NBA fans, too. Team locker rooms have big-screen TVs that let players, like the Nets' Kenyon Martin, keep an eye on the competition. Players also watch videotapes of their opponents to help plan strategy.

CAN YOU SIGN, PLEASE?

These lucky fans caught Yao Ming of the Houston Rockets at his hotel before the 2003 All-Star Game. Autograph experts say that NBA players are more likely to sign for fans who are polite and friendly, so mind your manners!

KEEP YOUR PEN HANDY

Players will sometimes take a moment before games to sign autographs, too. Even though this young autograph-seeker is a Tracy McGrady fan (check out his jersey!), Jerome James of the Seattle Supersonics is happy to sign for him.

ALMOST THERE!

Here's something that very few fans get to see: an NBA player on the team bus, heading for a game. Teams take a bus from their hotel to the arena. Boston Celtics star Paul Pierce calls home on his cell phone as the team arrives for a game in Atlanta.

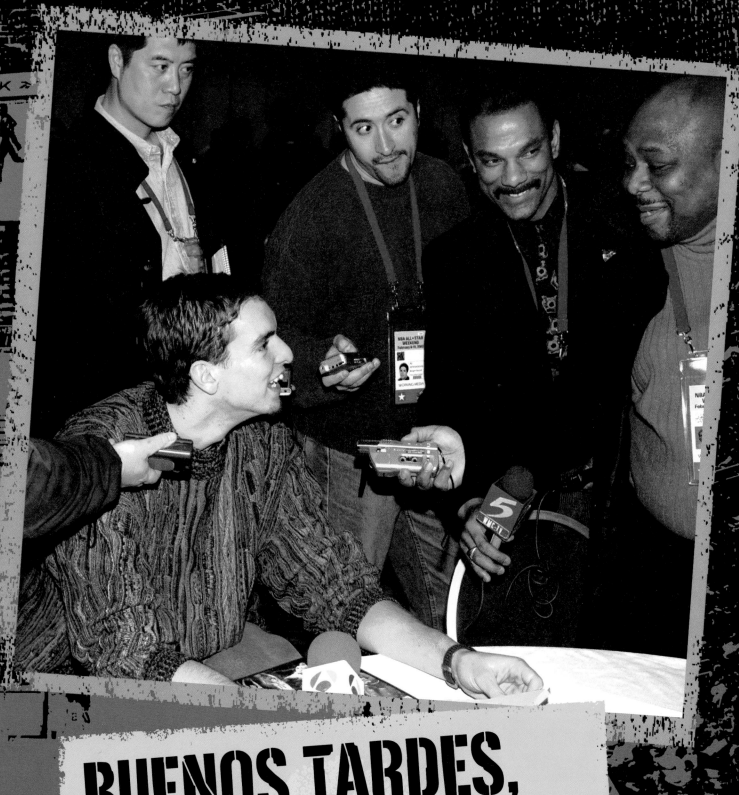

BUENOS TARDES, AMIGOS!

Doing interviews is part of life in the NBA, as Memphis Grizzlies forward Pau Gasol learns here. Interviews like these help fans learn more about their favorite players.

CALM BEFORE THE STORM

No admittance—except for you! Here's a sneak peak into the Rockets' pregame training room. That's Yao Ming enjoying a cold treat will getting his foot taped by assistant trainer Michelle Leget.

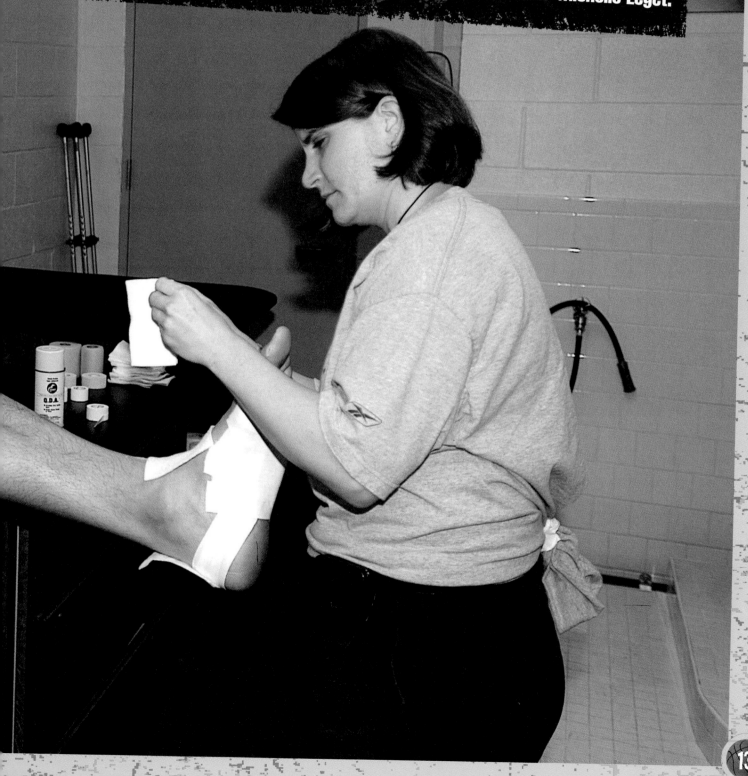

HA-HA, HOOPS!

Tony Parker of the San Antonio Spurs knows that playing in the NBA is hard work, but it's also fun. Here he is having a laugh before a game.

WORDS OF WISDOM

Coaches are always trying to help their players improve their game. During pregame warm-ups, Seattle head coach Nate McMillan delivers some key pointers to Rashard Lewis.

LOOK AT US!

Players aren't the only ones who get psyched up for a game. These Nets fans have obviously worked hard on their outfits, too. Hope they used washable paint!

REALLY BIG SHOE!

This young Lakers fan could probably use Shaquille O'Neal's size 22 EEE basketball shoe for a chair. Hopefully, he's planning to give Shaq back his shoe before the game starts!

HAIR'S LOOKING AT YOU!

Power forward Ben Wallace of the Detroit Pistons is famous for his powerful rebounding and jaw-dropping shot-blocking. He's also known for his wild hair-styles. Here he poses with some young fans sporting Wallace wigs and holding Ben Wallace bobblehead dolls.

STRETCH IT OUT

Brad Miller of the Indiana Pacers joins teammates stretching before a game. Players warm up carefully and stretch their muscles before a game. Young players should make sure to do the same!

HERE WE GO NOW!

Game time is just moments away . . . Dirk Nowitzki gets high fives from his teammates as he is introduced to the crowd in Dallas before a game against the Pistons.

OKAY, HERE'S THE PLAN...

When you win nine NBA championships . . . people listen! Coach Phil Jackson (who also won six titles as coach of the Bulls) goes over the game plan with Rick Fox and the Lakers. Phil and other coaches use erasable whiteboards to draw plays during games.

HUDDLE UP!

The New Orleans Hornets crowd in to get themselves psyched up just before tipoff. Basketball is all about teamwork, and moments like these help a team work and play well together.

TIPOFF TIME!

The 2003 All-Star Game tips off in Atlanta. The tipoff is only used to start a game and after jump balls. In early basketball, however, there was a tipoff after every point scored. Why? Because they hadn't come up with the idea of cutting the bottom off the basket! Someone had to poke the ball out of the wooden basket after each score!

WHAT'S SO FUNNY?

Players are not only teammates, they're often good buddies. They spend many hours together and have a lot of fun. Even on the bench, during a quiet moment in a game, they can take a moment and laugh at a good joke. Maybe the Spurs' mascot did something goofy!

INSTANT REPLAY

NBA referees, like Dan Crawford here, study videotape replays to see whether a shot was taken before the final buzzer of a period or a game. They can also check whether a shot was taken from behind the three-point stripe.

FIDO GETS BIG AIR!

NBA fans sometimes enjoy halftime performances like this by a Frisbee-catching dog in Phoenix. Notice that the canine high-flyer is wearing little rubber sneakers? If you've ever seen a dog try to walk on a wooden floor, you know why!

NEWS FLASH!
GIRL CAPTURES GIANT RED DINOSAUR!

Just kidding . . . This is only Raptor, the mascot of the Toronto Raptors. Many NBA teams use mascots to help entertain fans between plays and before and after games. Mascots also act as goodwill ambassadors for the teams, joining players on visits to schools and hospitals.

TIME FOR HARDWARE

Kevin Garnett answers questions from reporters at a press conference after winning the 2003 All-Star Game MVP. Players meet with reporters after every game to help fans learn not only what players do, but what they think and say. What would *you* ask Kevin?

MICROPHONE FOREST

Along with press conferences, players sometimes have to deal with a big media crowd. In moments like these for Kobe Bryant, it helps to be taller than your average radio commentator or newspaper reporter!

HERE'S TO THE WINNERS!

After a long and hard-fought game, there's nothing like being able to celebrate a victory! Just like fans in the stands and those watching or listening at home, players get excited when they win. Stephon Marbury of the Phoenix Suns celebrates a victory over the Spurs.